THE SIXTH CHOICE

A YA FANTASY ROMANCE STORY

M. L. BUCHMAN

Buchman Bookworks

I love Buchman's writing. His vivid descriptions
bring everything to life in an unforgettable way.

— PURE JONEL, HOT POINT

Other works by M. L. Buchman:

---

*H*artane the Younger hurried along the narrow cobbled streets, careful to dodge the droppings of burden beasts. A small pack of children, deeply involved in a game of Evade, stormed up and down the street, threatening trade and unwary pedestrians alike. Once clear of the mayhem, he crossed the street under the nose of a prancer awaiting its rider and climbed the six stone steps worn into soft curves by the generations that had climbed before him.

He squinted his eyes to block his wavering reflection in the mirrored front door of Cantel Kingdom's Lifemark Shop—not that there was anything wrong with the mirror, he just knew that "wavering" was how everyone saw him. As if he was as ill-defined as the blue, river clay molded by a child rather than shaped by a master potter.

But not after today. His seventh year began today. He'd at long last reached his majority. Choosing his

Lifemark today—the one special power that would lead him forward—would surely snap his life into sharp focus.

It just had to.

Sweat stung his eyes and his hand was shaking as he grabbed the cool brass doorknob—the only one he'd ever seen, perhaps the only one in the whole kingdom. Hartane had asked three separate people who had gone before how to operate it so that he didn't end up the fool trying to lift or push or slide. Grasp firmly and turn was the trick.

It squealed as he did so, a high-thin sound not unlike when he'd slipped a slimy, hand-long, densel slug down the back of his little sister's frock for teasing him until he…well, slipped a slimy densel slug down her frock. The sister-like squeal of the brass was the only sound he heard over the blood pounding in his ears. The rumble of the heavy carts and brutish six-legged burden beasts jarring over the cobbles, mere steps behind him, might as well have been off in some small village far away from the great capital city.

Actually…he truly couldn't hear them.

Hartane turned to observe the carts to make sure that they still moved, and though he could see the dust they raised and the beasts' weary manner, his racing heart was the only thing he could hear. His own fear-sweat was all that he could smell.

Curious, he released the knob he had only half turned and took the single step from the stoop of the shop back onto the cobbled street. The world slammed back to life about him. The dried dung, both fresh-dropped and the old, powdered by the successive burden beasts, tickled his nose until he sneezed. The clatter of ironwood wheels over hard stone was such a surprise he had to cover his ears at the suddenness of it. He backed up onto the stoop and hung onto the door knob for support, not trusting his knees.

Once again there was silence.

Now he was no longer sure that he was ready for this moment to be so momentous—for a single choice to shape his entire life.

He faced himself once more in the mirrored door.

"Pull yourself together, Hartane," he told his ill-defined reflection and could hear his father's inevitable words. "*...or you'll end up as no more than a burden-beast driver until the end of your days.*"

"*Pull yourself together, Younger,*" Hartane the Elder never called him by his given name. "*You'll be a man someday, though the Great Queen alone knows how.*"

The mirror reflected his own gray eyes, wide with nervousness, blinking like a nightbird spooked from its nest in the midday sun. But the mirror reflected none of the world behind him. In this place, only he existed.

Hartane did his best to square his shoulders, though his reflection was unimpressed by the efforts on his gangly frame. He pushed open the door. Now that he was seventeen, he could come as many times over the next cycle of seasons as he wished before choosing his Lifemark. However, he knew he would receive more of his father's heavy judgments if he did not choose soon and wisely. Delaying the matter, even past the midday meal, while he carefully considered the options was *not* an option.

He pushed open the heavy door and stepped into his future as boldly as he dared.

Again, he had asked many what to expect within. The shop both matched and didn't match the image he had built in his head.

Damal waved from behind a wooden counter that filled half of the small entryway. They barely knew one another. Growing up in his family's university housing, Hartane had little to do with the tradesmen of the village, especially ones who were many turns his senior.

"You have your letters, boy?" Damal's tone was like Hartane the Elder's, filled with doubt that he, the Younger, could have possibly achieved literacy. However, no matter the disdainful dismissal inherent in his tone, his question explained Damal's role here: to help those who didn't have their letters. When Hartane nodded his assent, Damal lost all interest in him.

Hartane had learned to read by the time he could walk. Had read widely in the Great Library of the Blessed Aramala. It required only a child's skill to read the simple words burned into the polished brightwood placard above Damal's counter.

Choose carefully.
A Lifemark that is too far from the soul
will have an ill effect at best.
A Lifemark that is too close to the soul
will be an opportunity wasted.

No more than a single Lifemark may be chosen.
Life is balance.
May Aramala guide your hand.

HARTANE SENT a brief prayer for wisdom to the Goddess. It sounded more like him begging to not make a mess of his choice, but it was the best he could manage.

Holding his breath, he finally turned to face the main room of the shop. It had lurked there, out of the corner of his eye, but he had not wanted to turn and gawk like some tweenling. Old Vanek, his tutor, had told him to read the sign carefully when he entered and consider it thoroughly before proceeding.

"No need to know what it says before you are ready," the old scholar had insisted. "But do not go quickly by." Vanek had guided much of Hartane's exploration of the library, so he had tried to let the ancient's wisdom guide him in this as well.

Old Vanek had never told him what Lifemark he had chosen for himself. "I shall not influence your thinking in these matters."

Hartane desperately wished he knew, but not even on Vanek's deathbed would he say.

He tried to honor Vanek's instructions and read the sign one more time, but he couldn't force himself to turn away from the shop's interior! It was magnificent.

Light shone down through clever windows in the ceiling, reflecting off white-mudded walls. Not the gray of stone or colorful with tapestries—stark, unblemished white. He'd never seen such a room, with the walls so smooth he wanted to reach out and touch them. But Hartane was very conscious of being the only person present other than Damal and resisted the urge.

The room was completely filled with shelves. From knee to eye-level, tiers of brightwood lined the walls. Down the middle stood even more rows. Rare brightwood, so precious that he had seen it but a few times in his life, was everywhere. The luster that glowed from within warmed the shop and scented it with memories of the air as clear as the high mountains on which it grew—he had to trust Mendal's word for that. He alone of all the people Hartane knew had traveled to the mountains for the hundred-year harvest.

Upon each shelf were long lines of baskets woven of simple wicketweed. The juxtaposition of the valuable and the mundane spoke that neither of those were what was important here. It was only the contents of the baskets that mattered. Each basket represented a single future—an enchantment that focused a person's mind and soul upon some particular skill so thoroughly that it could not be denied. To take one of the vials in the basket and drink it was to set a life's path. Nestled within each basket, snug among the glass-blown vials filled with vari-colored potions, rested a tiny, fired bowl of blue, river clay. Those were filled with colored slivers of paper —samples.

Though the shelves were separated into five sections around the shop, the array remained bewildering.

Practical
Creative
Community
Self
Universal

Each of the five major sections were broken down into subsection rows. It was as familiar as the library and as foreign as his father's office that held very few texts and much equipment.

By chance, the first basket he focused upon held the Lifemark his father had chosen: Mechanics. Hartane the Elder was the kingdom's master of the advanced design of mechanical tools. Force and its application were his father's great knowledge.

Hartane knew the expectation; Elder had been very clear on that point. Knew that Elder would then bend him to be his apprentice and had trained him all his days to that purpose. Even reviving the arcane custom of naming your offspring after yourself; Hartane the Younger was perhaps alone in his generation to bear such a burden.

Instead of instantly doing as his father would want, he turned and faced…the Warrior's collection.

It was a small act of defiance, one he knew he would not sustain but he felt lighter for it nonetheless.

Though he had turned from the Mechanical Skills category of baskets, he knew that was where he would end up after investigating all of the others. Still, it was his one chance for a view of other possible lives within the community and he was going to make the most of it.

He knew he was no warrior, but it was the furthest choice he could imagine from Elder's world. Rather than simply moving on, he selected the small strip of red paper from the tiny cup beside vials of the Spearman's Lifemark.

He slipped it into his mouth and let it dissolve on his tongue. There was a bitterness of unboiled tankar sprout and the sweetness of redberry. And for five long heartbeats he felt the power surge through him as if he stood far broader than he did. The enemy lay below and they would rue this day. And though his comrades-in-arms or even he himself might fall, the victory would be sweet.

On the sixth heartbeat the sample released him. Hartane looked down to make sure he was unchanged. Still slender and over-tall. Still awkward. Definitely not a good fit.

He looked to the next basket out of the hundreds that ranged down the shelves. There was only one way to be sure, but it was going to be a very long day trying every option in the vast shop.

He took the testing strip for a Tunneler and laid the cool earth-tasting paper upon his tongue.

---

2

*R*ania had entered the shop many times in the past, even though it was forbidden. This time felt no different except she used the front entrance rather than the back.

The mirror didn't reflect the carriage her father had sent her in, as if she was too frail to walk from the palace. It reflected only the face she washed each morning. Yet in this mirror it was changed somehow though she could not discern exactly how.

Her bright hair was tied back with a thin strap of Royal's-only blue tak-tak hide that matched her eyes. Her face was clear of blemish. Still…she was somehow different in this reflection.

With a shrug she turned the knob, so strange against the palm of her hand as if it too was changed. Or perhaps it merely was testing that her maturity had been reached. She breezed into the shop because this was her valid majority day. Not that it really mattered. *Princess following in parents' footsteps to a throne she wasn't interested in,* her life in a nittle shell. Besides, the queen was so healthy she'd probably live a hundred-year. If she did, Rania would be too old, and her offspring—required in the next five years or else—would take the seat in her place.

Damal greeted her with a knowing smile that she ignored and brushed by him into the shop. No more need to ever again tolerate his oaf-clumsy hands or rancid, fried-streamslipper breath overly hot upon her bare neck. He had served his purpose these last nights, letting her see the choices before the time of her majority. It had seemed important to be here before her time, though now she didn't know why.

Not that it mattered. She was half tempted to select Entertainer of Men simply to send the Great Queen into another of her spells; Mama had been breathing down her back for months about this.

And then she spotted Hartane the Younger among the baskets.

She hadn't known they shared a birth date. Rania sampled a creamy strip of Clothier while she watched him move from the martial arts to the building trade. His clothing was barely presentable, though before her sixth heartbeat she could see how a few adjustments might bring out the man in the boy's clothing.

When the sample faded, so did the idea of how to fix him up, but not the memory that it was possible. He had always been the strange one in the court crowd— stumbling almost as horribly over his own feet as he did over his words. His second home seemed to be in the palace library, so she saw him often even if they interacted little. He pursued the great texts of the ancients, she preferred the storytellers' tales in another section.

She'd roamed these aisles a dozen times, once she'd freed herself from Damal's overeager gropings, but no fate had suited her. Who needed a future Queen who could fish, understand the laws of numbers, or heal the injured?

Yet as she wandered this time, she could not help noting that Hartane the Younger was doing something other than mere sampling. He moved methodically from basket to basket, trying every one.

She watched him through grimaces, sweating, wide-eyed horror, and an odd fit of laughter that had him shaking his head for several moments after the effect of the sample wore off. Every now and then he would make a small note on a coil of paper.

"What are you doing there?"

His marker and paper coil sprang aloft from his fingers, but his hands were quick enough that he recovered the paper mid-air. The marker landed in a basket of Animal Healer vials. He retrieved it before turning back to his notes.

"Sorry, you startled me."

"Answer the question."

3

Hartane had not previously considered the possibilities of working with animals: handling, healing, or husbandry, and wished a moment to consider the implications though none of the three had tasted properly on his tongue. He knew that wasn't an essential element, but it was, he hoped, a strong indicator of being on the right path or not.

The Herder of Kattines had left him laughing. He'd wondered if even training would be possible. He couldn't imagine a single kattine, lying asleep in the sun, would have the least interest in being herded. Perhaps it had been created as a prank by the Queen's Fool—a bewildering man who seemed to have taken an especial joy in targeting Hartane whenever they met. At times it felt as if the man liked him. At others as if he was pitying Hartane, though—to use some of the Fool's alliterativeness—he certainly enjoyed pithing Hartane.

Ah, Younger. Are you ever planning to grow into your own feet?

Well, he finally had, but that didn't stop his still tripping over them on occasion.

He turned to the woman beside him and this time lost both his marker and paper coil to the floor. Bending down to retrieve them, he banged his elbow on a shelf setting off a thousand vials rattling together like his nerves.

He held his elbow as well as the unintended bow as he mumbled out, "My lady."

"Hartane," the Princess huffed out her exasperation. "Stop that."

"As you wish," he rose slowly, so that he didn't catch his elbow on the way up. Then had to bend back down to retrieve his marker and paper, like a popping-toy being pressed down and springing back up.

Toymaker, he hadn't thought of that possibility. Would that be in the Practical category or the Community one?

"What are you doing?"

He thought it was a little obvious, even for the Princess. He considered taking the Fool's role and offering a pedantic reply such as, "Picking my Lifemark." But instead he began babbling: much more his normal form.

"I'm sampling all the possibilities and noting compatibility trends based on sample color, temperament of resulting Lifemark alignment with my own natural taste profiles and…" He squinted at the Princess. "Why are you smiling?" He inspected his clothes, but he hadn't managed to damage his best attire—yet.

He looked back up at her. He'd never stood so close to Royalty, and definitely not to the Princess, the one True Heir. Her perfection was quite breathtaking and had been terribly distracting as she wandered about the library. She paced about as she read, often speaking the lines of the work—just to softly to hear more than the melodious whispers of her voice.

He'd sometimes wondered what she was really like, but that was his mother's skill. She could see the good in anyone and help them find it. A Mind Healer. He had tried to learn what he could from her, but that was so incompatible with his mental predispositions and Hartane the Elder's training that it rarely availed him any results. He'd spotted her Lifemark in the Universal section but the sample had tasted of nothing and he'd only felt disgust at what he'd then sensed from Damal the clerk—a desperate need to make himself feel superior to others, especially to those he knew he wasn't.

Hartane tried to see past the Princess' pampered skin, the golden fall of hair, and the bodice unlaced just the right amount to make the most of showing off her slender form. She was beauty. She would have power. Yet he could see…

"You are laughing at me, yet you are unhappy."

ania spun on her heel and stalked away.

Damal was smirking at her from a distance. Fine. She grabbed a vial of Entertainer of Men, but a hand rested lightly on her arm to stop her.

"What?" she ground out to Hartane the Younger who had followed her and touched her without permission. She didn't turn to face him, which left her glaring at Damal as he made a point of looking her up and down. Of course he would know the arrangement of the baskets and exactly what vial she had grabbed. Even as an Entertainer of Men she would never, ever give herself to him again. Not even for the mere kisses she had previously allowed.

"Do not choose in anger, Princess. Choose carefully. The sign says so."

"And you always do what signs say?" She turned her back on Damal. She pulled off the strip of blue tak-tak hide so that her long hair spread and hid her bare shoulders from him.

Hartane shrugged uncomfortably.

"So, what would you choose?"

"I have yet to sample all that is possible."

"Har-tane!"

"I would not choose that which my lady presently holds even if I were a woman."

Rania looked at the thin vial filled with viscous red fluid, that moved sluggishly as if it had no life. He would not choose it? In truth, neither would she.

She returned it to its basket, resisting the urge to slip it into the True Love one that lay close by—all bright and cheery in blossoming pink.

Metna the baker's son came in, greeted Damal, and, joking together in the way she'd heard tradesmen do, they headed down the aisle discussing what choice Metna should make: his mother was a chef, his sister made the best sweetgoods, perhaps Hunter of Animals for their table?

"If you are so wise, Hartane the Younger, choose for me then," Rania told him.

"I could not!" Hartane's protest was one of abject horror.

"And why not? You have clearly given much thought to this. More than I," she didn't enjoy admitting. Her time with Damal had all been a waste. She knew nothing, even less than the inventor's son. To take the bite out of her next words, she smiled upon him and liked the feeling of it. "Choose, I command it."

"You might as well command the stars, Princess." Hartane shook his head. "How could I choose but a single strength for our future Queen? She must have wisdom and heart and fairness. A keen sense of consequence. And—" he was rambling again.

Besides, a single choice was for the likes of him. Not her. He could feel his destiny lurking over his left shoulder. Elder's assistant, Elder's slave until his dying day.

He could taste the bitterness of it, far sharper than any words the Fool had ever laid upon his head.

No.

No! He would not take up his father's mantle. Just as the Princess should not take up the vial she had held, he would not take up Elder's. He felt suddenly adrift, unanchored. His whole life he'd known that ultimate answer to his choice. With that choice abandoned—

unless he weakened worse than he felt he might—his future suddenly had no anchor. A foolish metaphor for him, though he'd been testing the Seaman's trade when the Princess had accosted him. All he recalled was that it had tasted of salt and fish and the wildness of the sea. He and the outdoors shared only the most tentative of acquaintances. No, not the sea for him either.

"Hartane? I've have commanded you to speak, and yet you give me silence."

"Sorry Princess," he bowed deeply in apology, keeping an eye out for the edge of the shelf. As he arose, he noticed her slight smile. She'd been…teasing him? Rather than a monarch's harsh command. He tried returning the smile and liked the way it felt. Perhaps being the Queen's Fool would not be such a poor role after all.

"Your beauty will make people listen. Your wisdom and power will gain respect. But as the sign says, balance is what will make you beloved."

"What is this sign that so fascinates you?"

Hartane laughed in surprise, but the consequential scowl no longer scared him. The Princess saw none of the possibility of her future. None of the importance.

He offered his arm and escorted her back to the entryway until they stood once more before the sign. He could hear Damal make some insulting joke about his arcane manners, but with Princess Rania's hand resting lightly in the crook of his elbow, he was above such noise.

Choose carefully.
A Lifemark that is too far from the soul
will have an ill effect at best.
A Lifemark that is too close to the soul
will be an opportunity wasted.
No more than a single Lifemark may be chosen.
Life is balance.
May Aramala guide your hand.

"LIFE IS BALANCE, my lady. The Great Queen and her consort, your father, bring that balance. Some day it will be yours to bring as well."

She stared up at the sign for a long time and Hartane waited.

It was long enough that he could feel his "Younger" nerves struggle to resurface as if drowning in the great river. But this time he would not descend into those dark waters; he had the Princess on his arm. Even if only for this one moment, he was at her side.

Her voice was soft when she turned to look at him. So close that he could see the details of her irises as clearly as one of Elder's gear-workings pumps. "And what would you choose for yourself, Hartane?"

"I have not completed my study yet, Princess," he held up his coil of paper as if to prove his point.

"Okay. Let me try to ask you in your language."

"I have a language?"

"Shush," they were so close that her breath brushed warm upon his cheek. She was tall, as tall as he was. For reasons he could not explain, he liked that and wondered why he hadn't noticed it earlier.

He shushed.

"You say that it is wrong for me to choose any single Lifemark."

"It is. You mustn't…" Her elegant arching of her eyebrow said that she too had a language. He clenched his jaw against further speech.

"Yet your precious sign says that I may chose only one."

He eyed the sign: *No more than a single Lifemark may be chosen.*

"So tell me, and this is a command. If it is wrong for *me* to choose any single Lifemark, why would *you* choose to so limit yourself?"

"It isn't a limit. It's a…" But was it?

In his mind, a chasm opened before Hartane's feet right there in the entryway of the Lifemark Shop.

To one side stood all of his years of study, building up to this moment, this choice. Months of research. Perhaps years of worry and fear.

On the other side of this choice stood…what? Suncycle after suncycle of striving to be like his father? Ever seeking Elder's approval, knowing it would never come? Or—choosing a different future and earning Elder's everlasting disdain.

He looked over Princess Rania's shoulder at the five signs marking the five areas of the Lifemark Shop.

Practical

Creative

Personal
Community
Universal

She would need all of those and more. But how?

Once again he studied the entry sign hanging before them. "What if," it seemed a sacrilegious thought, "what if there is a sixth category?"

The Princess turned to gaze upon the shelves, "I see no gap. No sixth section."

"Exactly."

She squinted those lovely eyes at him as if he'd lost his mind.

Perhaps he had.

Still she waited.

Laughter once again rippled back and forth between the Damal and his friend. Hartane could feel it take root inside him, for entirely different reasons.

Laughter.

Not the dutiful laughter required by one of Elder's jokes—as meticulously planned and designed as one of his machines. Had Elder chosen Entertainer of Men, might he have been a troubadour rather than an inventor? His desire for joke telling far outstripped his skills in that area.

Nor was it the laughter that comes from slipping a densel slug down your sister's frock.

No, it was the laughter that started in the heart and welled upward, that sped up his pulse and made him dare smile upon the great beauty and future power before him.

"I shall not influence your thinking in these matters," he repeated old Vanek's oft-spoken phrase to the Princess.

"Then what are you doing, speaking of six categories when there are only five to be seen?"

"It is a message from an old friend. A very wise old friend who has finally answered my question though he's been dead for many seasons. Come, Princess," he offered her his arm once more. When she took it, he began leading her toward the door.

"But—" she tugged back lightly and pointed toward the arrayed vials.

"The sixth choice, my Princess, is to make no choice at all. No choice at all is still, as my beloved sign says, *no more than one.* Life is *indeed* balance exactly as the sign says. By selecting a Lifemark, we become very powerful in a single area. By selecting none, the few who understand and dare to follow that last instruction know that only as ourselves can we truly find that balance. It is a balance that a ruler needs and, though it be sacrilege, I expect your mother the Great Queen lacks. I would wish it for you."

At the threshold, with the door still open behind them, standing on the isolation of the front stoop, the Princess looked at him and whispered little louder than the beating of his own heart in his ears.

"Perhaps, Hartane the Wise, you should begin to call me Rania."

He could feel the smile grace his lips. Not premeditated. Not considered and practiced in hopes of appearing acceptable. His lips moved of their own accord and he felt no need to judge or guide them.

Together they stepped from the Lifemark Shop and the door swung closed behind them. Off the stoop, the world came to life and wrapped about them with open arms.

MONK'S MAZE (EXCERPT)

IF YOU LIKED THIS, YOU'LL LOVE THIS
SECOND DARK AGES NOVEL!

*B*rother Colin Clark's handlight slipped from his chilled fingers. It bounced once, twice, a third time, clattering loudly off the rocks in the quiet of the night, then went out.

He lunged for it and clipped his shin hard against a boulder.

"Blasted St. Nicholas." Tumbling forward, he crashed onto the ground.

His hands wrapped about his shin were filled with a sticky warmth. The only thing that wasn't freezing on this stupid planet. Why of all people had he been the one sent back to Earth? Many of the other brothers had been eager for the adventure.

"Let them," he'd wanted to shout when Brother David chose him as the Order's emissary.

"Let them be the ones sent to lie in the dark." But no, it was quiet, unassuming Brother Col who had to lie on the rough rock of this remote island with the pain rocketing up his nerve endings. Blinking his eyes did nothing to reveal even the vaguest of shapes in the overcast, moonless night.

"So don't lie in the dark." Brother David's cracked old voice was as clear as if he were right beside him rather than a memory that he'd left a dozen light-years behind on New Kells circling a friendly orange star.

"Okay, turn on the light switch." He gasped when he realized he was talking back to the old man. He ducked the scowl more fierce than a slap could be. A year in transit aboard ship and he still feared the old monk.

Besides, as far as he could tell, there weren't any light switches on Iona, or on the planet for that matter. Every observation he could make from orbit revealed no use of any broadcast media. No powered vehicles even.

"Find the handlight." Brother David was always full of orders, but he did have a point even if he was just a memory.

Colin rose to his good knee and addressed the darkness.

"I would greatly appreciate it if any crawlies or other nasties this planet has, would please move aside this night." His voice fell flat and was ripped away by the wind into the vast darkness.

He reached out with hands that retained little feeling and began to probe the cold, wet grasses and rough, rocky crevices. He poked about in a slowly widening circle.

His arm plunged elbow deep into a freezing puddle before he realized what was happening. He jerked back and caught his elbow on another blasted rock, rose to his knees only to put weight on his abused shin, and collapsed once more to the ground.

"Bloody hell!" He was in too much pain to bother being shocked by his own language. Flopping sideways in the grass he wrapped his good leg over his throbbing shin and a hand about the twinges shooting up his arm. He'd never found that particular bone to be the least bit funny. Though all the other brother's certainly delighted in how often he rapped it.

He needed shelter. Now. He needed to be back on the deorbiter, which was hidden in an old barn a kilometer away over rough ground. He needed a building, but he was completely lost in the darkness even before he'd dropped the stupid handlight. He'd take a stone wall right about now and be happy. Well, happier.

A drop of rain splashed on the bridge of his nose and spattered into both of his eyes.

"Father, Son, and the Holy Ghost!"

MEGHAN TAYLOR HAD BEEN STARING out the window when the light appeared. Appeared where no light should be. None could be. Nor was it the flickering light of flame, but bright and white and steady as no light should be.

For a minute, perhaps two, it wandered about the ruins of the abbey on Iona. Then, as she'd reached for the binoculars, it spun about and disappeared.

A minute passed.

Five.

Fifteen.

No light returned. No light on Iona.

Please, no light on Iona.

Had she been asleep?

No, it was sleeplessness that had brought her to the window in the night.

And her feet were far too cold against the chill stone floor of the Watcher's hut for it to be a dream.

She inspected the alarm panel. Fascinated even after a year by the glow of the steady lights that held no heat. There were no alarms from the abbey doors. None for the chapel. None for the bishop's house or even the abandoned village. Every light glowed a soft green. Steady, like the light on Iona she truly hoped she had not seen.

Her hand hovered over the red button. The one that would call the Guardians. That would bring to Iona the only authorized users of technology.

But what could she tell them?

"I'm, ah, fairly sure 'twas a light I saw."

"No. I dinna know what happened to it."

"It was late and I was na sleeping well." Too many thoughts of the fast-approaching end of her exile. Too anxious to head home in just five days.

"No. The wee light did na come back, but I dinna think I imagined it."

She moved her hand away from the red button and stared out at the darkness. She knew the view even on nights like this when there was none to be seen. A short grassy slope dropped from the front of her hut down to the rough waters of the Sound of Iona. Less than a kilometer away, across the dark water, Iona. The height of Dun I, the hundred meter-high mountain of the island, towering above the north end. Grassy meadows sprawling from shore to slope dotted with ancient stone buildings. All misted by the soft pattering of the light spring rain.

And the abbey. The abandoned home of the thrice-cursed Order of Iona.

For a year, well, three hundred and sixty days of it so far, she had watched the abbey until it loomed large even in her nightmares. And now, with just five days to go, there was a light where none should be.

But with nothing to focus on, her eyes shifted to her own, dim reflection in the window. She contemplated the disjointed collection of shapes lit by the ever-burning green lights of the panel.

Her face, thin and white, made gaunt and ill in the dim glow. Black hair lost in darkness. Not reflected at all.

Crossed arms over an invisibly dark nightshirt appeared connected to nothing.

Two dim trunks of legs appeared far below as if severed yet still standing.

Scattered pieces, all shivering in the chill that was as much inside her as against the bottoms of her feet.

Was she truly coming apart? Losing her mind as Mad Erin had half a decade before? A girl gone mad with the Watching of the most evil place on Earth. In the end speaking only to the gulls who cried forever above the rocky shores of Eilean nam Ban. The Isle of Women.

The cursed isle.

Her prison.

She closed her eyes.

Five days. Just five more days.

The madness circled about her on silent wings, swooping ever nearer.

Please let there have been a light.

ABOUT THE AUTHOR

M.L. Buchman started the first of, what is now over 50 novels and even more short stories, while flying from South Korea to ride his bicycle across the Australian Outback. All part of a solo around-the-world bicycle trip (a mid-life crisis on wheels) that ultimately launched his writing career.

Booklist has selected his military and firefighter series(es) as 3-time "Top 10 Romance of the Year." NPR and Barnes & Noble have named other titles "Best 5 Romance of the Year." In 2016 he was a finalist for RWA's prestigious RITA award.

He has flown and jumped out of airplanes, can single-hand a fifty-foot sailboat, and has designed and built two houses. In between writing, he also quilts. M. L. is constantly amazed at what you can do with a degree in Geophysics. He also writes: contemporary romance, thrillers, and fantasy.

More info and a free novel for subscribing to his newsletter at: www.mlbuchman.com

Join the conversation:
www.mlbuchman.com

Other works by M. L. Buchman:

The Night Stalkers

MAIN FLIGHT
The Night Is Mine
I Own the Dawn
Wait Until Dark
Take Over at Midnight
Light Up the Night
Bring On the Dusk
By Break of Day

WHITE HOUSE HOLIDAY
Daniel's Christmas
Frank's Independence Day
Peter's Christmas
Zachary's Christmas
Roy's Independence Day
Damien's Christmas

AND THE NAVY
Christmas at Steel Beach
Christmas at Peleliu Cove

5E
Target of the Heart
Target Lock on Love
Target of Mine

Firehawks

MAIN FLIGHT
Pure Heat
Full Blaze
Hot Point
Flash of Fire
Wild Fire

SMOKEJUMPERS
Wildfire at Dawn
Wildfire at Larch Creek
Wildfire on the Skagit

Delta Force
Target Engaged
Heart Strike
Wild Justice

White House Protection Force
Off the Leash
On Your Mark
In the Weeds

Where Dreams
Where Dreams are Born
Where Dreams Reside
Where Dreams Are of Christmas
Where Dreams Unfold
Where Dreams Are Written

Eagle Cove
Return to Eagle Cove
Recipe for Eagle Cove
Longing for Eagle Cove
Keepsake for Eagle Cove

Henderson's Ranch
Nathan's Big Sky
Big Sky, Loyal Heart

Love Abroad
Heart of the Cotswolds: England
Path of Love: Cinque Terre, Italy

Dead Chef Thrillers
Swap Out!
One Chef!
Two Chef!

Deities Anonymous
Cookbook from Hell: Reheated
Saviors 101

SF/F Titles
The Nara Reaction
Monk's Maze
the Me and Elsie Chronicles

Strategies for Success (NF)
Managing Your Inner Artist/Writer
Estate Planning for Authors